MW00880182

Timmy's
MONSTER
Diary

Property of Timmy the Monster.

Dedicated to Reya,
Charlotte, Arlo and Aurelia.

—R.M.

To William, who survived book two and created
garbageball. And to the Ithaca Ward Nursery
2016, the original Fire-Snakes.
—A.S.

To my parents, who let me draw all the time.
—J.H.

Copyright © 2017 by Raun Melmed and Annette Sexton
Illustrations copyright © 2017 by Jeff Harvey
All rights reserved.

Published by Familius LLC, www.familius.com

Familius books are available at special discounts for bulk purchases, whether
for sales promotions or for family or corporate use. For more information,
contact Familius Sales at 559-876-2170 or email orders@familius.com.

Library of Congress Cataloging-in-Publication Data
2017904492   ISBN 9781945547195

10 9 8 7 6 5 4 3 2 1

Cover and book design by David Miles
Edited by Katharine Hale

First Edition

AN ST4™ MINDFULNESS BOOK FOR KIDS

Timmy's
MONSTER
Diary

Screen Time Stress

(But I Tame It, Big Time)

by Dr. Raun Melmed

with Annette Sexton & Jeff Harvey, Illustrator

FAMILIUS

A Note About ST₄

As a developmental pediatrician, I see children every day with problems such as anxiety, poor self-esteem, ADHD, and even screen addiction. If only these children had a set of tools available to help them address these issues! From the literature and my own clinical experience, the Stop, Take Time to Think (ST$_4$) Series was born. Using this technique, children can learn to recognize the incredible strength they have within them—regardless of any special needs.

Imagine the sense of accomplishment that comes when children realize that they have the power to take charge of their own bodies and minds! Children can take a few moments before responding to stressful situations or acting impulsively. They can become attentive, aware, appropriate, and, in short, mindful.

The heroes, the tools, and the scenarios in this series are all designed to build self-awareness and self-esteem. Readers can watch the characters grow and learn to be present in the moment. Consequently, the characters see improved behavior, gain more friends, and build happier families—which are the goals for the children reading this series, as well!

Of course, these tools are only intended to be a part of an overall treatment program, but empowering children and their families to take charge remains key.

Good luck!

Dr. Raun Melmed

Contents

CHAPTER 1:

Game Over: Time Flies, Zaplet Dies

The ZugZug ate me. Again. Me, Timmy Tentacle. Beaten by a glob of pixels. I was SO close to finally beating Level 51 of Alien Universe. It's the best zaplet game since Doodle Quest. EVERY minor monster EVERYWHERE is playing it.

In the game, you're a monsternaut flying the most frightful spaceship, blasting alien ships, asteroids, and space cannons with lasers. You beat each level by flying to the planet at the end and defeating the evil alien Drago.

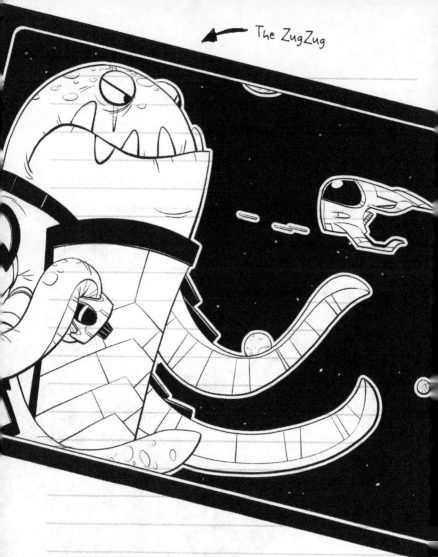

The ZugZug

It took me three months to beat the first 50 levels and unlock Level 51. That's where you meet the ZugZug. HUGE, with armor too thick for any lasers, the ZugZug chases and eats everything that flies past. Including my spaceship.

The ZugZug doesn't care how many rocket boosters I have. He is ALWAYS faster, and he is ALWAYS hungry. I've been working on Level 51 for a whole month. Tonight, I finally made it to Drago's planet, but I had to slow down for the space battle.

Game over. It's the furthest I've gotten since the time the twins swiped the screen and made me fly backward right into the ZugZug. Mom says baby brothers are better than zaplets.

I'm still not convinced.

Typical

I'm sure I could have beat Drago
tonight if I kept trying, but my
zaplet died and the charging cord
doesn't reach my bed. That might
be a good thing. It's already three
hours past bedtime and Dad says
minor monsters who sleep play
better garbageball.

I NEED to play some scaryific garbageball at tomorrow's game. If we win, we go on to the Monstertopia Championship! I still can't believe I'm on the Monstrocity Minotaurs team with my friend Marvin.

Marvin is the BEST at scoring cans, even if he isn't always a team player. He taught me to score my first double-can about a month before tryouts. That's when we became friends.

He's really my only friend on the team. I'm glad he'll be at the game tomorrow.

CHAPTER 2:

Time Out:
Time Is Out to
Get Me

I hope today's game goes better than
school. I failed my Monsterology quiz.
I had to stay in from recess to study.
Mrs. Grimm said she wants me to pass
the Monsterology test next week. I think
she just likes keeping minor monsters in
from recess.

Grimm strikes
again

I didn't turn in my fumeistry homework either and got a red spike sticker. If I get three red spikes this week, I'll have to miss recess again. I've been missing a lot of recess lately.

MINOR MONSTER MISHAPS								
LILY				TIMMY	💧			
NATE	💧			JERRY				
BROOKLYNN	💧			PAM				
PENELOPE				KELLY				
JACKSON				KEVIN				
KLINE				MARVIN				
OLIVE	💧			MICHAEL				

It's all Mrs. Grimm's fault.
She assigns too much homework.

Plus, she makes school so long and boring that I can't think when I get home. Yesterday I was so tired I HAD to play a level of *Alien Universe* to relax. One level wasn't long enough.

27 levels may have been too long, though.

Time is tricky. It always speeds up when I don't want it to. I wish it would speed up on the garbageball bus. Time ALWAYS goes slower on the bus. Today will be even worse because Marvin has a fangist appointment and his mom is driving him to the game.

I'll be on my own with Heidi, Helga, and Oscar for 30 minutes. It might as well be eternity. They snortle so loudly I can hear them through my earbugs. They're always saying, "Timmy, talk to us." "Timmy, be nice."

Felix and Harriet aren't quite so bad, but they do tell Marvin I'm not friendly. I AM friendly. I just like playing on my zaplet better than talking. The ONLY thing I have in common with my teammates is loving garbageball. It's the best game ever invented!

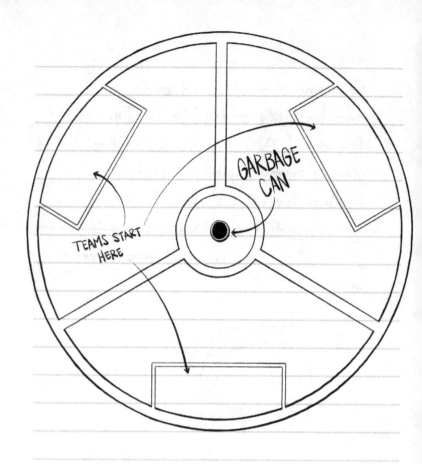

GARBAGE
CAN

TEAMS START
HERE

You play with three teams on a
terrorific circular court. Everyone
tries to get a ball into a garbage can
at the center to score. You score cans
and double-cans by throwing the ball
in, but bouncing the ball in gets you a
triple-can.

You can bounce the ball off the floor
or another player, but it's best to use
a teammate since an opponent might
steal the ball. Marvin is scary awesome
at triple-can bounce shots. I'm pretty
scaryific at assisting, but my favorite
part of the game is dribbling.

Scary player and
scary-awesome
friend.

Coach Gorgon says my tentacles give me a natural advantage when it comes to dribbling tricks. I hope my tricks work this game. They haven't gone well the last few practices. Yikes! The bus just pulled up. Garbageball game, here I come.

CHAPTER 3:

Game Time:
We Win, I Lose

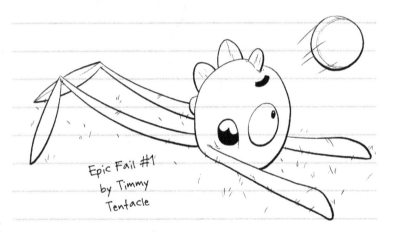

Epic Fail #1
by Timmy
Tentacle

We won! We're going to the Monstertopia
Championship next week! Dad might be
right about sleep, though. I played my
worst garbageball ever. I was so tired I
tripped over my tentacles a dozen times.

I missed nearly all my passes. I didn't score a single can. I dropped the ball while dribbling three times. The other teams stole the ball from me five times and bounce-scored off of me twice.

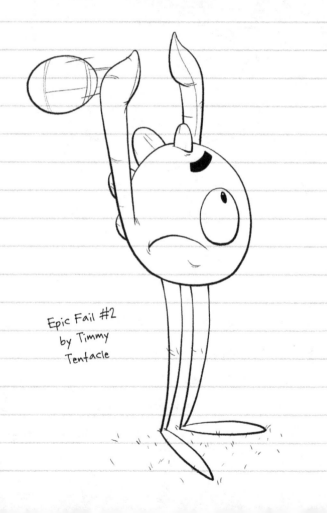

Epic Fail #2
by Timmy
Tentacle

I even messed up Marvin's triple-can
bounce shot by catching the ball when
he tried to bounce it off my tentacle.
I missed his signal and thought he was
trying to pass it to me.

Epic Fail #3 by
Timmy Tentacle

Worst of all, I didn't have my zaplet on the way home. Coach caught me playing *Alien Universe* in the second round and took it. We were winning by 20 cans. I thought I could play a quick level before I went in for round three.

I thought wrong.

Happy
me.

I lost the 20-can lead single-tentacled, and we barely won in the end. I think it was really Coach Gorgon's fault, though. Yelling puts me off my game. Coach is keeping my zaplet the entire bus ride back to school.

I haven't been without my zaplet since the time I caught the twins licking it like it was a dirty dinner plate. Mom put it on time out in the closet for a week because I yelled at them.

Double gross

I'm pretty sure I almost died that week.

This bus ride might be even worse, though. I have nothing to do except think about what Coach told us after the game. In the Championship next WEEK, we'll play the Creatureburg Beasts AND the Wyrmdale Fire-Snakes.

They're the only two teams to beat
us all season. The best teams in the
entire county! We've never played
both in the same game. The entire
team is nervous. They keep talking
about Coach's pep talk.

It went something like this:

You have the skills to be a great team, but you won't win next week playing like you played tonight. Winning the Championship is going to take every team member playing his or her BEST garbageball.

Then he pulled me aside. He told me
I'm a terrorific team player and scary
awesome at dribbling and passing, but
I've been distracted for months. He said
the team needs me to focus. Right. How
do I do that?

I REALLY don't want to let down
my team. They've all worked so hard.
I know I can play better than I did
today. Marvin offered to practice
extra with me after school tomorrow.
I hope it helps.

CHAPTER 4:

Practice Time:
I Try, I Fail
(Epic Fails 4-10)

Practice did NOT help. I never even
practiced. I forgot to go to Marvin's
house after school. I tried Level 51 on
the bus ride home.

Mistake. I was so focused on battling the ZugZug and replaying levels to earn fuel points, I completely spaced practicing with Marvin.

The whole day was bad, really. I missed the bus in the morning. I was bored waiting, so I popped in my earbugs and started an episode of *Super Scarers*. I didn't even hear the bus. Dad says I get distracted easily. Maybe he's right.

At school, I got a red spike for playing *Doodle Quest* instead of reading on my zaplet. I finished reading first, but class rules say no games. At all. Ever. If game sensing is a superpower, Mrs. Grimm has it. She always knows.

STER MISHAPS			
TIMMY	△	△	
JERRY			
PAM			

Timmy wins again! NOT.

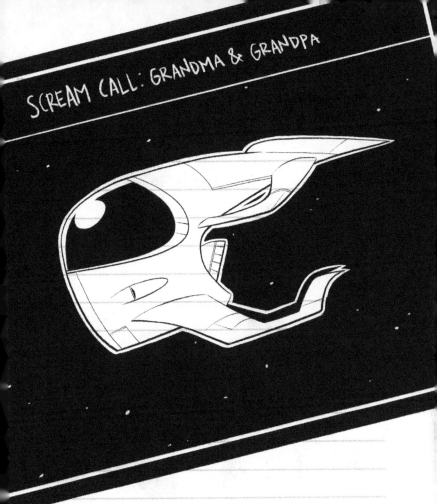

SCREAM CALL: GRANDMA & GRANDPA

After school was even worse.
Besides missing practice, I was
too busy playing games to notice a
screamtime call from Grandma and
Grandpa Tentacle. I haven't talked
to them in ages.

I didn't hear Mom ask for help making dinner, either. I missed out on making Gluten Globs! Then, during dinner, Dad lectured me about distractions because I didn't hear his question.

Luckily he didn't notice my zaplet at the dinner table. The twins noticed, though. They tattled on me because I wouldn't play snipe hunt with them.

No dessert for this minor monster.

It was my turn to lick the dinner plates clean, but I still hadn't done any homework. Definitely a case of time speeding up. I couldn't face more red spikes, so I decided to clean up later and started my double-fumeistry homework.

I forgot what sneezium was and had to look it up on Boogle. I spent the rest of the evening watching videos of exploding experiments.

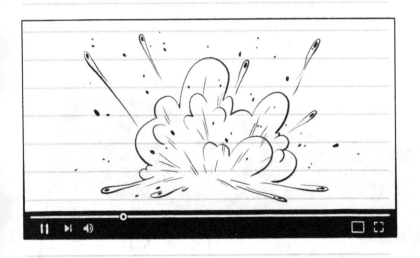

The dinner plates were still on the table this morning, and I didn't even finish my homework.

I definitely know what sneezium is
now, but that wasn't enough for Mrs.
Grimm. She still gave me a red spike
today for missing homework. My third
one, so I had to miss recess. Again.

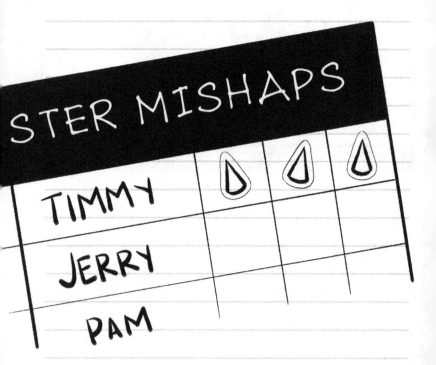

STER MISHAPS

TIMMY	◁	◁	◁
JERRY			
PAM			

This was the low point of the day. Then
Marvin asked to stay in from recess
with me. Marvin, the minor monster who
lives for recess! I was about to ask if
he needed the nurse when he spoke.

CHAPTER 5:

In the Club: Taking Time to Think

"Timmy, what's up with you? Red spikes? Missing practice?? Dropping the ball in a game??? You used to get gold spikes, and you're the best dribbler on the team. I need to tell you about ST 4. It keeps me out of trouble. I think it can help you too."

Marvin's 12-string baby fang guitar

"You remember how I used to miss recess a lot? I had trouble focusing. I forgot things all the time. That got me into trouble. Last year, I even forgot my 12-string baby fang guitar at home during the Minor Monster Music Fest! That's when I made up ST 4."

46

Marvin told me ST4 is a super-secret fumeical formula where the letters stand for words instead of smellements. The numbers tell you how many of each word you have. Marvin said I'm only the second monster to learn about ST4!

"S" means one word that starts with S, and "T4" means four words that start with T. ST4 stands for "Stop. Take Time to Think." When Marvin sees ST4, he remembers to stop what he's doing and think about whether it's what he SHOULD be doing.

Marvin told me he uses ST 4 every day, even for garbageball. ST 4 helps him remember to be a team player instead of just scoring cans. Without his team, he can't make the triple-can bounce shots. In fact, he never even tried a triple-can bounce before practicing with me! Monstrous.

Official club member!

Marvin made some badges to help him remember ST 4. I've seen them on his snapsack and three-claw binder. I've always wondered what they were. Marvin helped me make my own ST 4 badge for my zaplet. He says I'm in the ST 4 club now.

When my classmates came in from recess,
Mrs. Grimm had us pull up *Number
Munchers* on our zaplets and work through
ten problems. I got stuck on problem five.
I was about to give up and open *Doodle
Quest* when I saw the ST 4 badge.

I sent my work to Mrs. Grimm's zaplet instead, and she helped me figure out where I went wrong. Each time I got stuck, ST 4 and Mrs. Grimm helped me. I finished all my problems and won't have math homework tonight. Terrorific.

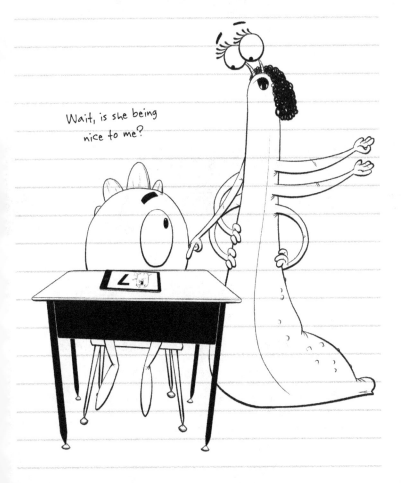

Wait, is she being nice to me?

On the bus ride home, I turned on
Super Scarers while the other minor
monsters talked about weekend plans.
The ST 4 badge reminded me to turn
my zaplet off at the end of the bus
ride instead of staying plugged in.

I headed straight to Marvin's house
for garbageball practice. We mostly
worked on dribbling to get me back
into shape. I tried to get to the can,
and he tried to get the ball away.

I dropped the ball a
few times but got to
it before Marvin each
time so he couldn't steal.

When I went home to start homework, I saw ST 4 again. I stopped before turning on my zaplet and decided to try my homework without it. I finished way more fumeistry homework than I expected but still had three words to look up on Boogle.

I watched one video of a flaming
fluorscream experiment before seeing
ST 4. I stopped, took a minute to think
. . . and decided I didn't need a video to
understand fluorscream. I looked up the
last two words without distractions.

Even though I don't use a zaplet for writing, staying focused on Meanglish was harder. Writing is exhausting, and reading Shakeshield is confusing. It was SO hard not to take a break for a quick zaplet game.

Each time I got tired of
Shakeshield, the ST 4 badge
stopped me from turning the
zaplet on just long enough to
think about Mrs. Grimm. I
finished writing the Meanglish
paragraph.

SUPER grim. I know which is worst.

CHAPTER 6:

Taking Charge:
I Clock, I Win

ST 4 seemed to be working. Even though I hadn't played any games since reading time at school and REALLY wanted to bring my zaplet to dinner, I decided to ST 4 one more time.

I stopped in my bedroom doorway with tablet in tentacle and thought about what Mom and Dad want me to do at dinner.

They always say they want family talk. I put the zaplet back on my desk and thought of something to tell my family.

Still double gross. But TERRORIFICALLY FUNNY!

At dinner, I told everyone about practicing garbageball with Marvin. The twins started dribbling frog eggs around their plates. They're kind of funny. With no zaplet, I wasn't distracted when Dad offered to practice with me too.

That's when I realized . . . I used to play garbageball almost every day with Dad! Until *Alien Universe*. I got so busy with Level 51, I stopped practicing with Dad, with Marvin, even on my own. I'm sure that's why I started playing worse in garbageball.

I started wondering what else I was missing out on because of spending so much time on my zaplet. The ZugZug wasn't just eating my spaceship—the ZugZug was eating my time.

My zaplet was eating my time.

I want to have time for garbageball
(and sleeping), Super Scarer figures,
Monsterman comics, Stickybrick
building, screamtiming grandparents,
cooking with Mom, crashcar mechanics
with Dad, even playing with the twins.

☑ Garbageball
☐ Super Scarers
☑ Monsterman
☑ Stickybrick building
☐ Screamtime with Grandma + Grandpa
☑ cooking with MOM
☐ Crashcar with DAD
☐ Play with TWINS
☐ Sleep

I decided to take charge. Mom, Dad, Coach Gorgon, Mrs. Grimm, even Marvin have tried to help me, but I am the only monster who can decide how much time to feed my zaplet.

I have to choose when to use it and when to put it away.

When I WANT to use my zaplet, ST 4 can help me stop, think, and choose to spend time on something else instead. When I SHOULD use my zaplet for school or homework, ST 4 can help me use my zaplet the right way and for the right things.

Either way, I still feed my zaplet too
much of my time, even with ST 4 to
help. I decided to try a timer to limit
my zaplet time. I'm not sure why I
didn't think of it before. There's a
timer right on my zaplet!

I set a ten-minute timer and pulled up *Alien Universe*. I figured I could get through five levels in ten minutes. I couldn't see the timer while playing, though.

After two levels, the timer buzzed so loud I threw the zaplet over the couch.

Flying zaplet

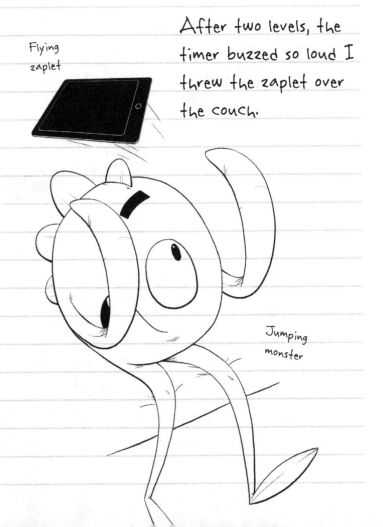

Jumping monster

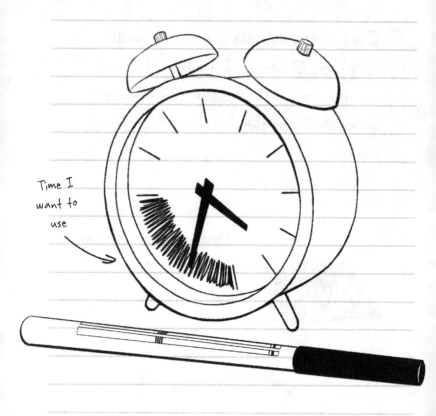

Time I want to use

I needed something visible. I got the clock from my room. With an erasable marker, I drew one line at the minute hand and another line fifteen minutes later. I colored in the space between the lines. Perfect. Just call me Albert Slimestein.

I set another zaplet timer and tried
to get through five levels again, but
this time I watched the time clock
too. I could see the minute hand
tick from the first line to the second
line and didn't jump when the timer
buzzed.

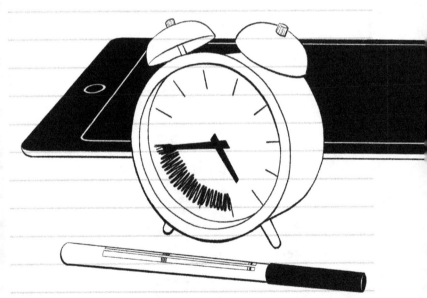

Finished time and
NO jumping monster!

My next idea

TIME LOG		
ACTIVITY	TIME EXPECTED/TIME SPENT	HOW MUCH I LIKED IT

I still only got through three
levels, though. The timer worked,
but I had no clue how long I
really spend doing things. I have
a reading log for summer to know
how long I read each day. I
decided to start a time log.

CHAPTER 7:

Timmy Time:
My Day, My Way

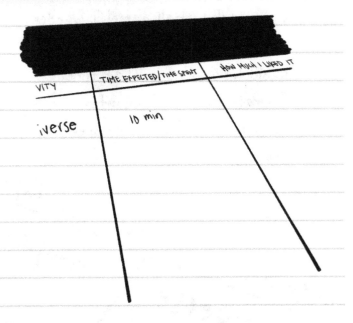

VITY	TIME EXPECTED/TIME SPENT	HOW MUCH I LIKED IT
iverse	10 min	

I wrote down "Alien Universe" and "10 min" for how long I wanted to play. I got my time clock, but this time I only drew a starting line. I played all five levels, then added an ending line. I colored the space in between to see how long I REALLY played.

It took 25 minutes to play five
levels! That's almost two rounds
of a garbageball game! I wonder
how many practice dribbles I
could have done in that time.
I wrote down "25 minutes"
for how long I actually spent
playing.

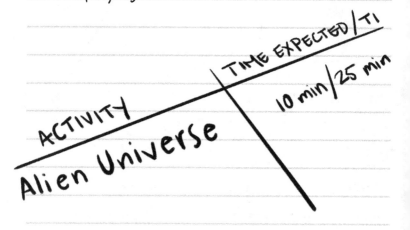

ACTIVITY: Alien Universe

TIME EXPECTED/TI: 10 min/25 min

I used my time clock and time log
the rest of the weekend to figure out
how much time I spend on all the
things I like to do.

I spend way more time
than I think on almost
everything. Thank badness
I have my time log now!

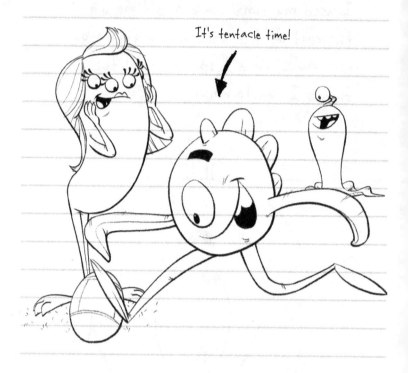

My favorite part of the weekend
was practicing garbageball. Marvin
invited the whole team to join in, and
they all really pushed me to dribble
better, especially Helga and Oscar.
They're scaryific blockers.

We also worked on some new triple-
can plays. Felix dribbled backwards
to Heidi, who somersault-passed
to Marvin, who overclaw-bounced
the ball off Harriet's head, off
my tentacle, and into the can.
Monstrous. Frightful. Terr. or. ific.

SCORE!!!

Frightfully cool person to talk to!

What surprised me most, though, was talking with them. I've always been too busy with my zaplet to do that. Helga and Felix love Monsterman Comics, and Oscar and Harriet have the same Super Scarer figures as me. Harriet even has a few I don't have.

Marvin left practice first. He said,
"I can't go another minute without
my 12-string baby fang guitar. We
usually rock all weekend together."
He spends the most time doing what
he loves best. It made me think.

Garbageball took more time than
I planned on my time log, but it
really felt worth it. I thought
about all the time on my zaplet.
It didn't feel the same. I wasn't
spending the most time on what
I loved best.

| reading | 30 min / 30 min |
| garbageball | 30 min / 1 hour |

TIME LOG		
ACTIVITY	TIME EXPECTED / TIME SPENT	HOW MUCH I LIKED IT
rbageball	30 min / 1 hr	10
zaplet	20 min / 30 min	6

I added a new column to my time log
to record how much I liked what I
did. I put a 10 for garbageball and
a 6 for zaplet games. I added scores
for everything else, too, so I can
spend more free time on the things I
like most. It felt scaremazing to be
in charge!

CHAPTER 8:

Monstrous Monday: Taming Time (Big Time)

I had the most monstrous Monday I've had in a very long time. I was almost excited to go to school. I knew I had all my homework done. I knew I was ready for garbageball practice. I knew I had used my time the way I WANTED to.

Who's prepared again? THIS GUY! AGAIN!

I chose to spend my bus ride talking
to Harriet about Super Scarer
figures instead of playing on my
zaplet. It felt great to have a new
friend. In class, Mrs. Grimm gave me
a gold spike for using my zaplet the
right way all day. Thank you, ST 4!

Team garbageball practice went
great too. I completed all my passes,
didn't drop the ball, and even scored
a can. Heidi, Felix, and Harriet tried
a couple of dribbling tricks I taught
them. Coach Gorgon was impressed.

After practice, I studied for the Monsterology test. I put my zaplet away in my room where it wouldn't be distracting and wrote "2 hours" on my time log for how long I thought I needed to study. I read over my notes three times and answered all the review questions!

I had the twins help me
with flashcards too.

An hour and a
half in, I REALLY
felt like I knew
Monsterology, and
I even got some
exercise. I wrote
down "1 hour, 30
minutes" on my
time log. For once, I
had time left over!
Scare. maz. ing.

TIME L	
ACTIVITY	TIME EXPECTED
Studying	2 hrs / 1 hr 3

I used the extra time to build a
Stickybrick spaceship. It looked
scary awesome . . . until the twins
found it.

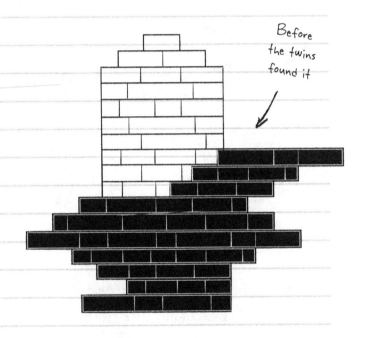

Before
the twins
found it

They prefer spaceships in pieces. Lots
of pieces. I didn't want to waste time
fighting, so I decided to play with them.

We played monsternauts and aliens.
They LOVED being ZugZugs and eating
my ship. When we had to clean up, they
pretended to eat all the mess in the room.
I told them where to put the things they
"ate," and they kept at it until the room
was clean. I barely did anything!

That's when it hit me: the ZugZug can HELP me defeat Drago by eating him, just like the twins helped me clean up! After dinner, I pulled up Level 51. Instead of blasting, I flew AROUND the ships and asteroids. With monstrous skill, I even flew around Drago!

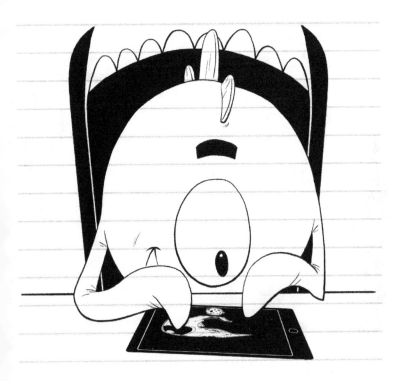

The ZugZug ate them all! Even Drago!! I tamed the ZugZug just like I tamed my zaplet. Both are terrorific tools, as long as I'M in charge. With the help of ST 4 and my time clock, I didn't play too long and even decided to go right to bed when I finished.

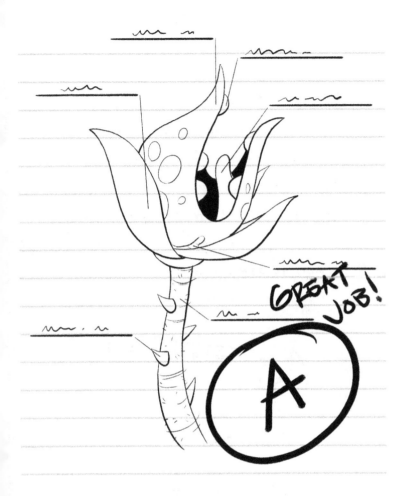

As monstrous as Monday was, Tuesday was even better. I passed my test! Thanks to ST 4 and my time clock, I studied AND got enough sleep. I answered every question and even knew all the parts of a fire-breathing snapdragon plant.

Now it's Wednesday. Game Day.
The Monstertopia Championship is
here at Monstrocity Middle School
this year, so no bus for us. My
friends (wow, that feels scaryific!)
and I are waiting for the other
teams to get here.

Felix just told a frightful joke, but
I was too nervous about the game
to laugh. Whatever happens with the
game, at least I know I passed my
Monsterology test. If we lose, maybe
I'll still have a future growing fire-
breathing snapdragons.

CHAPTER 9:

Monstrocity Minotaurs: Time to Play!

Part ogre and HUGE!

The Creatureburg Beasts won the first tip-off. Their jumping player is part ogre. Heidi never had a chance. He threw a double-can straight in. Oscar caught the rebound and underclaw-passed to Marvin, who gave me the bounce-shot signal.

SCORE!

I snapped my tentacle into position just in time to bump the ball into the can. Three cans! We were winning! Until the Fire-Snakes scored. We didn't score the rest of the first round. When the buzzer rang, the score was Fire-Snakes 12, Beasts 9, Minotaurs 3.

Second round, I subbed out. Helga, Harriet, Oscar, and Marvin played some scary-awesome garbageball. The Fire-Snakes and Beasts still played like the best teams in Monstertopia, but we were right up there with them this time.

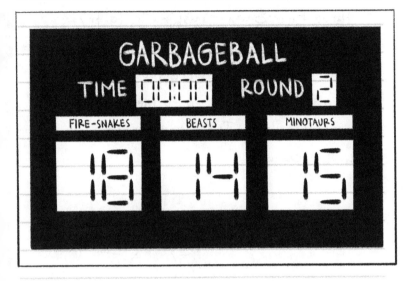

At the end of the second round, we were only down by three. We paid for it, though. Helga was out with a wing spasm, Oscar had a sprained tail, and Marvin took a bad bounce to the head. The Fire-Snakes won the third-round tip-off, but I caught the rebound.

There were two Beasts on one side and three Fire-Snakes rushing in to try a three-on-one blocking steal. Felix, Harriet, and Heidi were too far away to pass to. It was up to me. I pulled a pretzel dribble. The other players never had a chance.

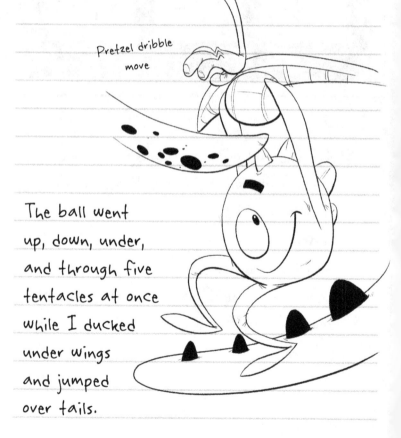

Pretzel dribble move

The ball went up, down, under, and through five tentacles at once while I ducked under wings and jumped over tails.

I passed the ball to Felix and gave him the bounce signal. He flipped the ball straight back to me and bounced it off my head into the can. Triple-can! It took new levels of teamwork, but we managed to keep our score up with the other teams.

SCORE AGAIN!

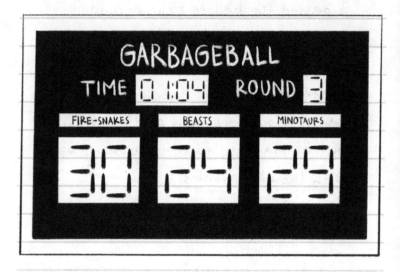

The last minute of the game, we were
only down by one can. Felix missed
a double-can. Harriet caught the
rebound, but the Beasts were closing
in. I dodged around the part-ogre
player to give her an opening, and she
dribbled, danced, and dodged just like
I taught her.

Then I had the ball. There were only seconds left, and the best scorers were out of the game. I thought back to my hours practicing with Marvin and hoped my scoring practice on Tuesday would pay off. I threw the ball up over the part-ogre player's head, over the can, and . . . straight into a Fire-Snake's wing.

Not this time, ogre!

Lucky for me, he was as surprised
as I was. The ball bounced off his
wing, straight into the can! I scored
my first-ever triple-can bounce
shot. The third-round buzzer rang.
The Monstrocity Minotaurs won the
Monstertopia Championship!

SCORE
AGAIN!

Just playing in the Championship was an easy 10 on my time log. Winning felt more like a 50.

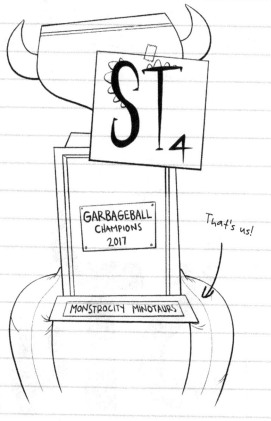

As our team went up to get the Monstertopia Chalice, I couldn't help snortling to myself when I saw an ST 4 badge on Marvin's claw.

Watch out Monstearth!
Timmy Tentacle and his scaremazing
time clock just joined Marvin the
Monster on a quest to Stop, Take
Time to Think!

Make Your Own ST₄ Badges

Ask an adult to help you photocopy these ST₄ badges.
Color them however you'd like, cut them out, and then
tape or pin them wherever you need a reminder!

Resources for Parents and Teachers

Let's face it: our children are using mobile devices earlier and spending more time than ever in front of screens. As with any technology, that comes with both benefits and risks. It is that risk-benefit ratio that parents must balance to help their children successfully navigate digital media.

Parents often feel poorly prepared as to how to address issues of time management and too much screen time, especially when things start to get out of hand. Screen-time trouble has parents worried—in fact, it is a universal concern in my practice. "How do I get my kids to stop? It's driving us crazy." Well, there's no need to go crazy, but there certainly is a need for guidelines.

Parents need to take the helm, and children need to play their parts as well. In this book, we address the needs of elementary-aged children, but the principles apply to all ages. We focus primarily on time awareness, which is one of the important underpinnings to living mindfully with technology, but we also discuss safe use of media and how parents and children can work together to create a better digital experience.

What Is Digital Media?

Digital media or *electronic media* are terms which are often used interchangeably. They can be defined as media accessed on a digital electronic device. They include software, digital imagery, digital video, video games, web pages and websites, social media, digital audio, and e-books. Digital or electronic media are frequently contrasted with print media, such as printed books, newspapers, and magazines.

Extent of Digital Media Use

Our society has become more dependent on digital media use. A recent study reported that by the age of 4, up to 96 percent of children used mobile devices, with some children starting before the age of 1. By age 2, most children use some type of mobile device daily!

In another study, by the ages of 3 to 4, most children were using mobile devices without any help—and a third of them engaged in media multitasking, which has been linked to task inefficiency in both children and adults.

This media use is not always child driven. For example, 70 percent of parents reported giving their children mobile devices to keep them occupied while they did household chores; 65 percent say they used mobile devices to keep their children calm; and 29 percent reported using mobile devices to put their children to bed. Other parents report using mobile devices as "digital pacifiers," to calm or to reward.

While TV screen time has decreased in recent years, mobile device usage has quadrupled in children aged 2 to 4. The American Academy of Pediatrics (AAP) has recognized the ubiquitous role that media plays in children's lives and now recommends that for children younger than 18 months, all electronic media other than video chatting should be avoided.

If electronic media is introduced to children 18 to 24 months of age, parents should choose high-quality programming. For children ages 2 to 5, screen use should be limited to 1 hour per day of high-quality programs. For those 6 years and older, the AAP recommends that limits are needed both on time spent using media and on the types of media. They suggest that children of any age benefit most when a parent acts as a "media mentor," meaning parents should use media with their child as much as possible and always be aware of what their child is doing online. For elementary school–aged children, this might mean discussing online safety and modeling healthy media habits. They go on to recommend that "screen-free" time should be designated for older children.

Are There Advantages to Screen Time?

Our children have unprecedented access to wonderful educational opportunities through digital media. Interactive, nonjudgmental apps can enhance cognitive development (processing and organization, visual spatial awareness, pattern recognition, and even reading), social and emotional awareness, and even moral development.

Apps for language development, academic enhancement, executive functioning, and creativity abound. Sure, parents must be selective, but there are resources available to help. (See "Common Sense Media" below.) For grandparents and other loved ones living further afield, video chatting has changed the landscape. It is not always easy to maintain a toddler's attention to a talking head, but with a little creativity, funny hats, and finger puppets, it's a marvelous way of staying in touch!

The more ways parents and children can interact around digital media use, the better. When a child reads a book, or even listens to an audiobook, they use their imagination to "picture" the stories—a creative process! While listening, if they follow along with a printed copy, that might also enhance their reading decoding ability and sight vocabulary. Using both digital and non-digital media together is a great way to benefit from screen time.

Are There Disadvantages to Screen Time?

We have all read horror stories of cyberbullying and sexting, and an excellent parenting resource on the subject is provided below. But what about the impact on basic functions such as sleep? What about the way screen time takes away from play time and family time?

Children today get less sleep than their predecessors, and it is likely that digital media is a contributing factor. More time on screens at night, along with the stimulating nature of the technology and the very content of the programs, will lead to less time sleeping. Is that a concern? Absolutely! Poor quality and inadequate sleep can result in inefficient cognitive processing, mood lability, irritability, and sluggishness—not to mention the impact on diet and weight gain.

There are apps that can teach the rules of social functioning. However, much of socialization takes place on the playground through typical play and the "school of hard knocks." If screen time takes the place of those opportunities, there is a concern that a child might become socially isolated and less socially adept, especially those children who already have social communication challenges.

As a developmental behavioral pediatrician, I commonly get asked if excessive screen time may lead to ADHD. While this is unlikely for many reasons, there is a concern that children with ADHD might be more vulnerable and more susceptible to excessive and problematic screen-time use. Children with ADHD can over-focus on highly stimulating tasks, making disengagement and transitioning to a more mundane task that much more difficult. Their high degree of impulsivity can lead to socially inappropriate online activity, which only serves to compound the challenges.

So What's a Parent to Do?

As mindful parents, we need to ask ourselves, what kind of parent are we, or even what kind of parent do we *want* to be? Surely we want to be able to instill self-confidence in our children and foster their resilience while enhancing their self-esteem and building their self-reliance. We want our children to participate in monitoring their own behaviors—especially when we are not around—and to make good choices. To do that, we must figure out how to balance being able to set rules while being flexible and allowing—nay, *encouraging*—our children to participate in the process. We would probably prefer to be less restrictive, not just by adopting a *laissez-faire* attitude towards parenting but by coming to the process with warmth and love, armed with good information. All children are inherently different; that's why the authoritative parent individualizes their approaches when there is more than one child in the family.

We must learn more about digital media and how to tame it. Armed with knowledge of the digital landscape, we can formulate a meaningful plan and, in so doing, be the parent we want to be.

Family Screen Plan

The first step in managing screen time or technology in the home is to come up with a "Family Screen Plan." Maybe appoint an "Information Technology Officer" who would champion the process. The plan should be reviewed regularly at family meetings to allow for flexibility and opportunities for individualizing approaches.

Setting the Tone

Paramount to the process is looking at the role of parents in setting the correct tone. Children model their behavior based on what they see. Parental engagement and social-ization with peers are critical—and sadly, we see examples of the opposite all too often. Ever walk in a park and see a mom or dad on their phone while their toddler runs about, attempting to engage their parents but eventually quieted with a device of their own?

It will likely take sitting down with all the family and creating some ground rules or activities for the Family Screen Plan. For example, consider taking a screen-free challenge by designating thirty to sixty minutes each day—aside from meal times—where the entire family unplugs together. That's tough: no phones, no laptops, no screens! You might even decide on a full day without screens, say a Saturday or a Sunday! What a wonderful way to model empowerment and family values.

Other planks in the "Family Screen Plan" could include guidelines for time spent on screens.

- Limiting media use to 1 hour a day for children 2 years and older.
- Setting up and keeping to the time set aside for screens—and for turning all screens off!
- Designating homework time as being screen-free, unless required.
- Reviewing homework before technology can be used. No rushing!
- Unplugging sixty minutes prior to bedtime for ele-mentary-aged children.
- Establishing clear time limits for screen-time use and using a timer to monitor compliance.

Screens at Meal Times

Screens should not be allowed at meal times. Screens at the dinner table are often the source of stress for all. Instead, switch it up and make meal time fun! It takes a little thought and preparation, but the more interesting the time around the table is, the more likely children will join in and participate in discussion and family time!

Ask your child to draw cartoons or cut out newspaper articles or comics to bring to the dinner table, and don't forget to participate yourself! Choose a theme for a meal once or twice a week such as colors or countries. Dress up, prepare by creating decorations, cook a special dish from a country, wear a funny hat, or eat outdoors at the park. Take meal times back!

What Else Can a Parent Do?

Avoid using screens or media to calm children down, except under extenuating circumstances!

Keep Screen Time Age-Appropriate

Parental oversight on their children's use of the internet and all digital media is imperative. It is the job of parents to protect the kingdom of childhood. Remember, protecting your child is a parental responsibility, not an invasion of the child's privacy. Check the Entertainment Software Rating Board (ESRB) ratings and select appropriate games—both in content and level of development. Play video games with your children to experience firsthand the game's content.

Screen-Free Alternatives

The Family Screen Plan should focus on alternatives to screen time and ways of creating a stimulating, creative, and fun environment. Children report they play video games, watch TV, or go online because they are bored. You cannot be your child's entertainment director at all times, but after-school programs and playdates will lessen boredom while allowing less time to end up on screens.

Distraction is an excellent strategy to use when observing negative behaviors. Keep a "Creativity Jar" close at hand with fun activities to play with, such as pipe cleaners or even shaving cream! Include simple, card-based trivia games or even a joke book. Distraction provides a way to avoid a media-heavy afternoon. Here are more ideas for "Creativity Jar" activities:

- Bake cookies; prepare fun fruit kebabs

- Create arts and crafts: string macaroni, finger painting, daisy chains

- Build an indoor fort

- Visit the library

- Prepare an outdoor picnic lunch or dinner

- Play cards or a board game

- Design a family Coat of Arms

- Go on a treasure hunt!

Activities That Timmy the Monster Uses

There are several activities that Timmy the Monster uses to ensure his time is well spent. The first is the ST_4 process, which was introduced by Marvin the Monster in *Marvin's Monster Diary: ADHD Attacks! (But I Rock It, Big Time)*. ST_4 is designed to enhance mindfulness and self-awareness. It gives children a tool for changing a situation by being mindful, thereby allowing them to have more control over their bodies and minds. They are engaged in the treatment process as team members, and this assures them that adults are on their side and that we do understand the challenges they are experiencing.

The **ST_4 process** works as follows:

1) Let your children know that they can learn the power to control their bodies, their arms and legs, what comes

out of their mouths, and even their thoughts! That is empowering!

2) Explain what a "formula" means, like how water is H_2O or oxygen is O_2. Use those as examples, but if that concept is abstract, just stick to the numbers and letters.

3) Tell your child how Timmy uses ST_4. They can keep the formula secret if they want.

4) They can learn to slow down and **S**TOP what they are doing—that's the **S** in **S**top. One **S**.

5) Now they need to **TAKE TIME TO THINK**. Count the **T**s—that's four, right?

6) One **S** and four **T**s—That's why we say ST_4.

7) Draw that formula on stickers or badges, then place the stickers on backpacks, on folders, on school desks, on the bathroom mirror!

8) It can be helpful to tell teachers about ST_4, as they might use it in the classroom as well. The teacher simply points to the sticker on the child's desk as needed. Keeping it secret allows the child to develop a positive rapport with the teacher while avoiding any unnecessary humiliation by being called out publicly.

The Time Clock

Awareness of the passage of time is invaluable for successful time management. Being able to tell time on an analog clock will help a great deal but is not essential for keeping track of time. So how can your child learn how to use the "Time Clock" like Timmy? Buy a glass-faced analog clock, often found in office supply stores, along with a packet of dry-erase markers. Color in a segment of time, say 15 minutes, and have the child focus on the minute hand, watching as it slowly moves through that colored 15-minute segment.

This can be used as a time awareness tool for homework or for time allowed on screens, videogames, or TV. When the minute hand moves beyond the segment, time is up.

Start giving warnings fifteen minutes prior to shutdown. Give reminders as needed every five minutes. A regular timer is another great tool which can help with transitions, and Timmy uses that as well.

The Time Log

This is especially good for homework. Some children feel overwhelmed when looking at their assignments; it can seem as if their work will never get done. We need to break it down for them. Draw three columns on a sheet of paper. The first column should be headed "Task Required," the second should be headed the "Estimated Time" the child or adult thinks the task will take, and the last column should state the "Actual Time" the task took.

For example, let the child guesstimate how long their math assignment will take. Write "Math" in the first column, and then the estimated and the actual time the task took. We all under- or overestimate how long things take, and in the case of ADHD, the swings in time estimation are even wilder!

Similarly, keep a log of how much time is spent on screens. Timmy uses his time log to see what activities he enjoys most, and he chooses to spend time on those activities. Let your child enter the activity, how much time they decide to spend, and then how long they actually spent. They are in for a revelation!

Conclusion

We hope that by being aware of our parenting styles, sensitive to our children's individualized needs, and armed with innovative tools, all our children can become confident, savvy, and mindful consumers of digital technology.

Resources

Common Sense Media: www.commonsensemedia.org

Establishing a Family Media Plan: www.healthychildren.org/
   MediaUsePlan

Learn to stop cyberbulling: www.stopbullying.gov

Learn more about children and media:
- www.pbs.org/parents/childrenandmedia
- Gold, Jodi. *Screen-Smart Parenting: How to Find Balance and Benefit in Your Child's Use of Social Media, Apps, and Digital Devices.* New York: The Guilford Press, 2014.

What Else Could We Do?

Check out these sites for more ideas and innovative screen-time alternatives:

- **Parenting** www.parenting.com

- **PopSugar Moms** www.popsugar.com/moms

- **Real Simple** www.realsimple.com

- **Babble** www.babble.com

- **Today's Parent** www.todaysparent.com

- **Better Homes & Gardens** www.bhg.com/health-family/
parenting-skills/

- **BuzzFeed** www.buzzfeed.com/parents

- **Good Housekeeping** www.goodhousekeeping.com/life/
parenting/

- **Family Education** www.familyeducation.com

- **Scary Mommy** www.scarymommy.com

About the Authors and Illustrator

Dr. Raun Melmed

Raun D. Melmed, MD, is a developmental pediatrician in Phoenix, Arizona. He is director of the Melmed Center and cofounder and medical director of the Southwest Autism Research and Resource Center. Originally from South Africa, he completed a fellowship at Children's Hospital Medical Center in Boston, where he was an instructor at Harvard Medical School. He is the coauthor of *Succeeding with Difficult Children* and *Autism: Early Intervention*, and he recently authored *Autism and the Extended Family*. He is a principal investigator of novel agents in the treatment of autism, Fragile X, and ADHD and collaborates on studies of tools used in the diagnosis of autism spectrum disorders.

Annette Sexton

Annette Sexton graduated from Brigham Young University with a BA in English. Diagnosed with ADHD at age ten, she is excited to help kids face and overcome some familiar challenges. Annette also studied music and enjoys playing the piano and French horn. She loves reading, crocheting, and being a mother to two beautiful, busy little girls. She lives in Ithaca, New York, with her husband and their two daughters.

Jeff Harvey

Jeff Harvey grew up in northern California doing nothing but making art. Since then, he has graduated from BYU in illustration and moved to Utah where he lives with his wife and family, still doing nothing but making art.

About Familius

Welcome to a place where heart is at the center of our families, and family at the center of our homes. Where boo-boos are still kissed, cake beaters are still licked, and mistakes are still okay. Welcome to a place where books—and family—are beautiful. Familius: a book publisher dedicated to helping families be happy.

Visit Our Website: www.familius.com

Our website is a different kind of place. Get inspired, read articles, discover books, watch videos, connect with our family experts, download books and apps and audio-books, and along the way, discover how values and happy family life go together.

Get Bulk Discounts

If you feel a few friends and family might benefit from what you've read, let us know and we'll be happy to provide you with quantity discounts. Simply email us at orders@familius.com.

Website: www.familius.com
Facebook: www.facebook.com/paterfamilius
Twitter: @familiustalk, @paterfamilius1
Pinterest: www.pinterest.com/familius

FAMILIUS

The most important work you ever do will be within the walls of your own home.

CPSIA information can be obtained
at www.ICGtesting.com
Printed in the USA
FSHW011436280121

9 781945 547195